WHEN YOU ARE LONELY

Tori Comes Out of Her Shell

JAYNE V. CLARK

Editor

JOE HOX

Illustrator

Story creation by Jocelyn Flenders, a homeschooling mother, writer, and editor living in suburban Philadelphia. A graduate of Lancaster Bible College with a background in intercultural studies and counseling, the Good News for Little Hearts series is her first published work for children.

New Growth Press, Greensboro, NC 27404
Text copyright © 2019 by Jayne V. Clark
Illustration copyright © 2019 by New Growth Press

Cover/Interior Design and Typesetting: Trish Mahoney, themahoney.com
Cover/Interior Illustrations: Joe Hox, joehox.com

ISBN: 978-1-948130-76-9

Library of Congress Control Number: 2019945101

Printed in Canada

26 25 24 23 22 21 20 19   1 2 3 4 5

"I am with you always."

Matthew 28:20

It was fall—a season of change.
The sound of chirping crickets turned to the sharpening of pencils.
It was time for a change for the Turtle family too.
They had grown out of their log home in Woodland Pond,
so they moved to Mulberry Meadow.

Their new log home had
plenty of room for Papa, Mama,
Tomas, Ted, and Tori.

On their first day in their new home,
the young turtles all sat outside on
a rock. They stretched their striped
arms and necks and enjoyed the
warm sun.

"Look, Ted!" Tomas shouted, pointing across the pond.
"I see some new friends! Race you!"
And they were off.

Left behind, Tori tucked her head
and legs deep inside her shell.
Now she looked just like the rock.

"Tori, where are you?"
called Mama coming out from the kitchen
and looking out over the pond.

Finally spotting her, Mama said,
"What are you doing out here all by yourself?"

"Nothing,"
Tori replied.

"Well, come inside and we'll make sure everything is ready for your first day of school! Just think of all the new friends you're going to make!"

But Tori wasn't so sure that making
new friends would be easy.
What if no one talked to her?
What if she had no one to play with at recess?

Or even worse, what if someone
made fun of her for being
"slow as a turtle"?

"Come on," said Mama.
"Let's pick out your outfit for school
and get your backpack ready."

"Okay," said Tori. She didn't tell Mama how worried she was. After Mama left, she spent the rest of the day by herself, unpacking her shell collection.

The next morning, they left for school.
Ted and Tomas saw their new friends, Buster Bunny
and Henry Hedgehog, up ahead and
caught up with them.

Tori straggled behind.

At school, Tori was welcomed by her teacher, Miss Minnick,
who asked Tori to introduce herself to the class.

Tori pulled her head into her shell.

Miss Minnick again asked,
"Can you tell us something about yourself, dear?"

Tori's voice echoed from inside her shell,
"I'm Tori from Woodland Pond."

Miss Minnick peered into Tori's shell and said,
"Thank you, Tori! We're so glad you're here at
Mulberry Meadow School. Please take a seat."

Soon it was recess time. Tori sat by herself, head tucked into her shell, watching the group that was jumping rope.

All she could think about was the time at her old school when she tried jumping rope only to trip and land on her back. She could still hear everyone laughing as she struggled to get herself right-side up.

She didn't want that to happen again!

Miss Minnick walked over to Tori.
"Wouldn't you like to play with the others?" she asked.

"No, no thank you. I'm fine,"
said Tori, peeking out from her shell.

Miss Minnick said, "I know it's hard
to go to a new school. When I was a kit,
I moved to a new town and realized I was
the only skunk. I felt so lonely. On my first
day of school, the fire alarm sounded by
mistake, and my worst fear was realized."

"Oh, no!"
Tori said.

"That's right.
I sprayed.
I sprayed my new desk, my new classroom,
my new teacher, and all my new classmates!"

"What did you do?" asked Tori.

"I didn't know what to do, so I just put my head down and jammed my hands into my pockets. But I found a card in one of them that my papa had given me. It was a verse from the Great Book that said, 'There is a friend who sticks closer than a brother.' It reminded me that Jesus would always be my friend no matter what."

"I thought I would never have any friends after that, but I'll always remember how Sally Salamander came right up to me and said, 'Don't worry. Everyone is afraid of being embarrassed. I'm afraid of sliming my chair.'

"Wasn't that kind of her? And we are still friends to this day."

Reaching into her pocket, Miss Minnick said,
"You know, Tori, I've had this for a very long time, but I'd like you to have it."

She pulled out the tattered card her father had given her long ago and handed it to Tori. Then she rang the bell to call everyone in from recess.

That Sunday, Mama, Papa, Ted, Tomas, and Tori went to their new church in Mulberry Meadow.

Tori looked up and right behind the preacher in big gold letters was a verse from the Great Book, "Jesus says, 'I am with you always.'"

All week Tori had been thinking about what Miss Minnick had said about Jesus always being her friend and here it was again.

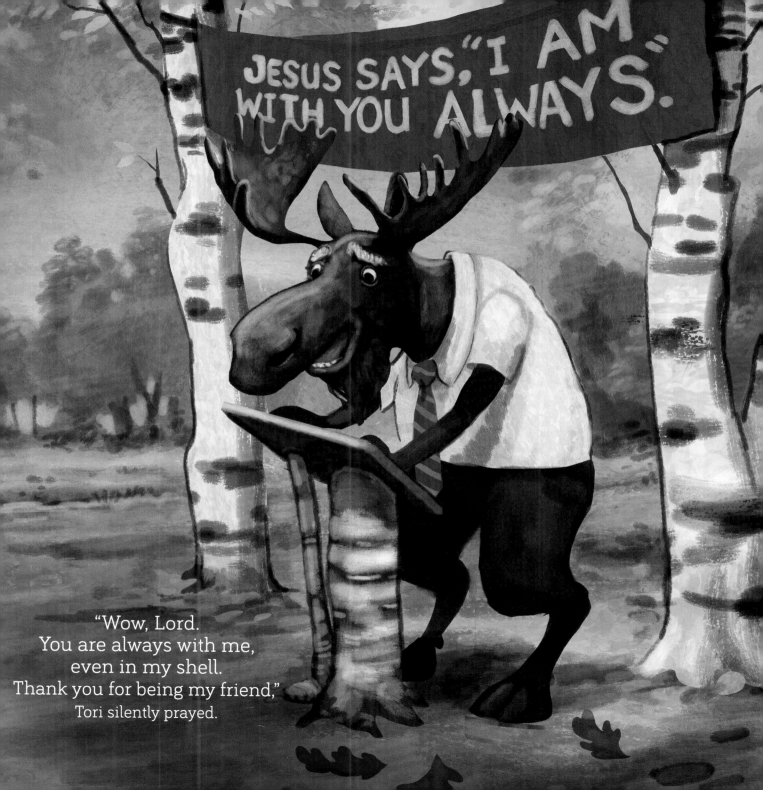

JESUS SAYS, "I AM WITH YOU ALWAYS."

"Wow, Lord.
You are always with me,
even in my shell.
Thank you for being my friend,"
Tori silently prayed.

Monday morning at recess, Tori was hiding her head in her shell again. She still didn't want to try jumping rope.

All of the sudden she noticed something shiny moving across the playground. Looking closer, she saw it was the top of an old school bell with legs poking out from under it. Whoever was in there was having a hard time walking.

Tori stuck her neck out and slowly walked over to see if she could help.

"Um, hello?" she said. "Are you okay in there?"

The bell became completely still.

Tori said again, "Hello, are you alright?"

Finally, two eyes peered out from under the edge and a voice called, "Yes, I'm fine. No need to worry."

"Are you sure?"
Tori asked.

"Well, maybe," came the reply.
"Could you lift this off me?"

"Sure. Do you need help
carrying it somewhere?"

"No, no, that's okay. I was just . . .
I was wanting . . ."

Lifting up the bell, Tori could see
that it was Gertie Gecko.
"What did you want?" asked Tori.

"A shell like yours. Ever since I saw
you in your shell during recess,
I wanted one too," said Gertie.

"You wanted a shell like mine?
Why?" asked Tori, surprised.

"Sometimes I feel lonely and I don't know who to play with at recess. I wanted to have a shell like yours to hide in. Even if you're all by yourself in there, I bet it always feels full. So I found this bell to use, but then I got stuck."

Gertie couldn't believe all that had just come tumbling out, but she did feel better telling someone.

Tori wanted to laugh. Gertie did look funny under that bell.
But then she remembered how it felt to be lonely.

"I do like to hide in my shell sometimes. But it gets awfully lonely in there.
I'm finding out that hiding is not the answer.
Maybe after school I can tell you what I've been learning."

"Would you?" asked Gertie. "That would be wonderful."

After school Tori and Gertie walked home together. While they were walking,
Tori took out the card that Miss Minnick gave her and read it with Gertie.

There is a friend who sticks closer than a brother.

"Jesus is always with me and he is with you too," Tori said.
"So even if I think I don't have any friends, Jesus is my friend?" asked Gertie.
"Yes," said Tori. "The preacher told us that God sent his Son Jesus
to this earth to make sure that we are never alone.

When you ask him for forgiveness, he becomes your friend forever."

Gertie and Tori walked home arm in arm. When they got to Tori's log, she asked Gertie, "Would you like to come in and see my shell collection?"

"I would love that," said Gertie.

"I can give you a shell of your own, but don't try to wear it! You aren't a turtle, you know."

This time Tori did laugh and Gertie laughed right along with her.

As Gertie was leaving, Tori invited her to come to church with her. Gertie said, "Yes!"

The next Sunday, the whole Gecko family squeezed into the pew with the Turtles.

Gertie poked Tori and pointed to the verse on the wall, "Jesus says, 'I am with you always.'"

JESUS SAYS, "I AM WITH YOU ALWAYS."

Tori whispered to Gertie, "See I told you so!
You can believe whatever the Great Book says!"

Tori and Gertie sang their new favorite hymn with their heads
held high—so high they could see Miss Minnick on stage
with the choir, smiling back at them.

*Have faith in God
when your pathway is lonely.
He sees and knows
all the ways you have trod.
Never alone are the least of his children;
Have faith in God, have faith in God.*

Helping Your Child with Loneliness

Some children love to be around lots of people, and others like to spend more time by themselves. Nothing wrong with that! But there is a difference between being alone and feeling lonely. Loneliness is a feeling of being isolated and disconnected from those around us. Sometimes when we feel lonely we are being ignored by people, but other times it's the fear of being rejected that keeps us from moving toward people. When that happens, often we react by isolating ourselves even more—by pulling into our shells, just like Tori does in this story. How do you help your child with this common struggle? Here are some biblical truths to share with your children when they are feeling lonely.

1 **Begin by sharing your own experience of loneliness.** Everyone has struggled with feeling isolated and alone. Let your child know this is a common struggle you have also experienced. Ask your children questions about why they might be feeling lonely. What happened? What might they be afraid of? Listen closely to what they have to share.

2 **Loneliness started with Adam and Eve.** We learn in Genesis 3 that when we go our own way and not God's way, the result is separation from God and from others. When Adam and Eve decided to disobey God's one rule, they broke their relationship with God and with each other. The first thing they did was hide from God, and then they blamed others for what they had done (Genesis 3:8, 12–13). Ever since, people have lived apart from God and one another. The result is loneliness.

3 **The cure for loneliness starts with a new relationship with God.** When Adam and Eve hid from God in the garden, God came to them. His first question to Adam and Eve, "Where are you?" was also Mama Turtle's question to Tori when she was hiding. God wants to be in relationship with his people, but our sins separate us from God and others. God knew we couldn't come out of hiding on our own, so he sent his Son Jesus to be with us, to love God and others, and then to die in our place so we never have to be alone again. The Bible says, "there is a friend who sticks closer than a brother" (Proverbs 18:24 ESV). When you ask God to forgive you for going your way and not God's way, then Jesus becomes your best friend. Jesus promises us, "I am with you always" (Matthew 28:20). That means he will always stay close!

4 **When you see your children hiding, you can remind them that because of Jesus, God knows them and sees them.** Tori's loneliness made her feel invisible. She was hiding in plain sight in her pond and in the schoolyard. Long ago there was a lonely woman named Hagar who had to leave her home. God found her in the desert, spoke to her, and promised to help her. Hagar was so amazed at God's care for her that she gave God a name—"the God who sees me" (Genesis 16:13). In Psalm 139, David reminds us that God is with us wherever we go and whatever we do. He sees us in the dark. He is with us every morning. He holds us fast even when we go far away from everyone else we know. It is a wonderful passage to read all the way through with your child.

5 **The only safe place to hide is in Christ.** When we hide from others, we are trying to keep ourselves safe—from rejection and the possibility of being hurt. But can we protect ourselves? We can't, but Jesus can. He is our all-powerful God who is with us. He sees us. He sticks closer than a brother. He is the one who will protect us from all harm. Jesus calls himself the good Shepherd. He promises to always watch out for his sheep. He will even give up his own life to keep his sheep safe (John 10:14–15). Jesus is our hiding place, who always protects us from trouble (Psalm 32:7).

6 **When Jesus is our friend, we become part of his big family.** The Bible says, "For God knew his people in advance, and he chose them to become like his Son, so that his Son would be the firstborn among many brothers and sisters" (Romans 8:29). When God is your father and his Son Jesus is your brother, your family includes all those who love Jesus. You and your child can know God's love through God's people, just like Miss Minnick loved Tori by noticing she was feeling lonely and sharing her back-pocket Bible verse with Tori.

7 **Love others the way you have been loved.** When we know Jesus loves us, that gives us the courage to move toward others and love them too. Jesus's friend John puts it this way: "We love each other because he loved us first" (1 John 4:19). As Tori learned, Jesus was her friend who was always with her and helped her notice Gertie, who was also feeling lonely and afraid. Knowing God's love brings us out of our shells and helps us to love others the way God loves us. Encourage your children to notice the "Gerties" in their lives and to think of ways to share God's love with them.

Back Pocket Bible Verses

I am with you always.

Matthew 28:20

You are the God who sees me.

Genesis 16:13

There is a friend who sticks
closer than a brother.

Proverbs 18:24 (ESV)

I will never leave you;
I will never abandon you.

Hebrews 13:5 (ICB)

For you are my hiding place; you
protect me from trouble.

Psalm 32:7

Lord, you have seen what is in
my heart. You know all about me.

Psalm 139:1 (NIRV)

Back Pocket Bible Verses

WHEN YOU ARE LONELY

WHEN YOU ARE LONELY

GOOD NEWS FOR LITTLE HEARTS

GOOD NEWS FOR LITTLE HEARTS

WHEN YOU ARE LONELY

WHEN YOU ARE LONELY

GOOD NEWS FOR LITTLE HEARTS

GOOD NEWS FOR LITTLE HEARTS